In The Pines

PRAISE FOR *STORYSHARES*

"One of the brightest innovators and game-changers in the education industry."
– Forbes

"Your success in applying research-validated practices to promote literacy serves as a valuable model for other organizations seeking to create evidence-based literacy programs."

- Library of Congress

"We need powerful social and educational innovation, and Storyshares is breaking new ground. The organization addresses critical problems facing our students and teachers. I am excited about the strategies it brings to the collective work of making sure every student has an equal chance in life."
– Teach For America

"Around the world, this is one of the up-and-coming trailblazers changing the landscape of literacy and education."
- International Literacy Association

"It's the perfect idea. There's really nothing like this. I mean wow, this will be a wonderful experience for young people."   - Andrea Davis Pinkney, Executive Director, Scholastic

"Reading for meaning opens opportunities for a lifetime of learning. Providing emerging readers with engaging texts that are designed to offer both challenges and support for each individual will improve their lives for years to come. Storyshares is a wonderful start."
- David Rose, Co-founder of CAST & UDL

In The Pines

Jennie Ford

STORYSHARES

Story Share, Inc.
New York. Boston. Philadelphia

Storyshares
Story Share, Inc.
24 N. Bryn Mawr Avenue #340
Bryn Mawr, PA 19010-3304
www.storyshares.org

Inspiring reading with a new kind of book.

Interest Level: Middle School
Grade Level Equivalent: 3.2

9781642611588

Book design by Storyshares

Printed in the United States of America

Storyshares Presents

1

Suzanne let the screen door slam as she came bopping out of the house. She had a look of satisfaction on her face. She knew how much Papa hated when she slammed that door. She would give it a little extra shove, making sure the slam sounded like a shotgun blast ringing through the house.

Granny came out on the porch. "Suzanne, why do you want to upset your Papa?"

Suzanne kept walking, never looking back.

"Where are you going, Suzy?" Granny yelled.

"Nowhere," Suzanne yelled back. Granny stood in the door watching Suzanne make her way down our long, sandy drive. Granny had a cloudy look on her face. I hated Suzanne for worrying her.

Granny noticed me sitting in a sunny patch beside the well. I had been up before daybreak. I was always an early riser. Everything was simple before the sun came up. I got up and went in the house.

Papa, my grandpa, was sitting in his recliner. He didn't stray very far from his recliner these days, or from his bottle of bourbon and his coffee cup that sat between his chair and the end table. I guess he thought it was hidden, but we all knew it was there.

"Where's your sister at?" he asked as I walked by.

"I don't know, Papa," I said.

"She's probably up to no good," he said.

I grabbed my tennis shoes from beside the couch and went on the porch to put them on. I didn't like being around Papa now. He had an old, sick smell. The kind of smell people get when they have lived past their usefulness.

Granny came out on the porch looking as fresh as the morning. It cheered me up. She had on her garden attire: flowered gloves, a big straw hat, and the long-sleeved plaid flannel shirt that hung on a nail on the back porch.

We made our way to the garden in silence. Wisps of wind sent the smell of ivory soap from Granny, who was walking ahead of me. I knew she was thinking about Suzanne.

Suzanne was a year and a half older than me. She was fifteen, and I was thirteen. She seemed much older. She hated being a child and tried her best to grow up quickly. She'd been giving Papa and Granny a fit all her life.

Our mother deposited my sister and me here before we were school age. We rarely saw her. When she died of ovarian cancer two years ago, it really didn't change our lives.

Mama had Suzanne when she was young. Mama ran away with our daddy at sixteen, breaking my grandparents' hearts. Suzanne was my Papa's favorite because she looked just like Mama.

Suzanne had dark hair, dark eyes, and olive skin. "Black Irish," Papa called her. I guess I looked like my daddy, although I could hardly recall what he looked like. I was strawberry blonde and fair skinned. My cheeks would stay bright red all summer long. Suzanne would turn as brown as a coffee bean.

Granny and I arrived at the garden. "It's going to be another hot summer . . . don't think I can take another one," Granny said.

She said this every summer without fail.

"You start in the peas. I'll get the squash," she added.

I began to chop the long rows of peas, hating Suzanne for not helping.

2

From my spot chopping peas, I could see my best friend Rose's house. It sat across a big, barren tobacco field. She had moved away well over a year before.

I smiled when I thought about Rose. We had known each other since first grade. I missed her so much. Rose lived with her father, who was an insurance salesman. Her mother was gone . . . that was all I knew. Not dead, just gone. I never asked where.

Rose was tall and skinny. She had long dirty blonde hair. It was parted in the middle and hung down her back. How I envied that hair. She was "shades" of pretty. Not pretty at first glance but pretty at certain times. She didn't smile very often.

Not at all like me who smiled too much, at everyone, at any moment. She reserved her smiles, using them only for a truly happy time. She wasn't the type to smile upon spotting me across the field, or meeting new people, or just for the hell of it.

Rose's father was tall and gaunt and wore black-framed glasses. He looked like a school principal. He was friendly and quiet. He had a nice, gentle face and sad, brown eyes.

I loved staying over at Rose's house on the weekends! It was so different from being at home. I felt worthwhile at her house, not "in the way." We would cook supper and wash dishes, fold clothes, and do "mother things."

Rose was used to it. It made me feel mature. Rose's father would bid us good night, and we would have full reign over the house. We could eat and stay up late.

Sometimes on hot summer nights, we'd take a cool shower and put on our cotton gowns. We'd sit on the porch with our hair wet and feel the cool air. We'd talk about life and boys. We'd talk of moving away to the coast. We'd imagine sharing a house and a dog called Rusty, named after the cutest boy in our class. We'd talk about this and sip coffee and "smoke" her dad's Winstons. We would stay out until the crickets quieted and all we could hear was the low breeze and an occasional owl in the woods.

I'd drift off to sleep in her bed and smile to myself and feel happy inside.

The day she told me she was moving, I cried. She was unemotional, as was her way.

"Dad is happy about it," she said. "Wilmington's a nice town. Dad will have more business. I'll miss you, Caroline." I continued my crying.

"You can visit me. It's on the coast!" Rose said with a rare smile.

"Yeah," was all I could say.

We both knew I'd never visit her. Even in our twelve-year-old minds, we knew.

The next Friday, the day Rose left, I was sitting on our back porch. The sun had just risen with a rage. I spotted her walking up the rows of the tall tobacco plants. She was smiling.

"Bye, Caroline," she said. "You will always be my best friend." She hugged me hard. She looked at me with her serious face. I saw tear drops. She turned and walked away.

Papa came out on the porch and saw her leaving. I tried to dry my eyes.

"Life is full of heartache, Caroline," Papa said, "but it goes on."

He walked past me to his truck. I smiled my best smile to his back. I realized then that I would never leave this place.

3

I was still staring off at Rose's house when Granny interrupted my thoughts. "Finish up your peas," Granny said. She was carrying a shirt-tail full of yellow squash. "And get your head out of the clouds."

I finished and went to the well and got a drink. I looked out across the sandy fields surrounding our yard. They were once full of big, green tobacco plants. They were once full of hot, sweaty workers. Papa was once one of the most successful farmers in our community. That was before his stroke. The stroke left him paralyzed on the left side. The stroke took away his spirit.

When Papa was farming, he and I would get up before the sun came up. God, I loved that time of day. The bright light in the kitchen made it seem even darker outside. I'd go to the porch and let the cool, damp air hit my face.

I could hear the chickens getting restless in the coop, the crickets still chirping just like it was midnight. The grass looked steamy and wet.

This was the best time for me. I was happy and glad to be alive this time of day before the sun came up, bringing with it the real world.

Papa would make us fried eggs, grits, and sausage. We'd warm up some of Granny's biscuits left over from supper.

"Us farmers got to start the day off right, don't we girl?" he'd say with a wink.

"Yes sir, we do!"

Papa and I would eat and then get in his truck and check the fields and barns already curing. "A fine crop this year," he'd say.

We'd go to the well and fill up the water tanks for the workers, then head into town for ice, sodas, and saltines.

I tried so hard to please Papa. I worked harder than anyone at the barns, looping tobacco until my hands blistered. I tried to do whatever he asked of me.

"Caroline, hook that trailer up over there and back it up to the barn so ya'll can unload it. I've got some business to take care of." Papa was talking to some men, agricultural men, I think. They were dressed too nice to be farmers.

I jumped on that tractor and worked the steering wheel and tried my damnedest to back up that long trailer full of tobacco. I felt the staring eyes. I knew all those men were watching. The more I steered and backed, the more nervous I got. I knew I couldn't do it, but in my ten-year-old heart, I'd do it or die.

I hit the side of the barn, tearing the tarpaper and spilling the whole load of tobacco. I looked at Papa and saw disgust in his eyes. The same look I got when I'd tangle my fishing line or cry or act too silly or stub my toe. This time, I also saw anger in his eyes.

I felt like Razzy Gentry. I didn't know who she was, but I'd heard her name all my life.

"If you don't get that frown off your face, it'll stick and you'll be ugly as Razzy Gentry. If you don't behave, you'll turn out meaner than Razzy Gentry. If you don't quit eating, you'll be as fat as Razzy Gentry."

Right then, I felt like the meanist, ugliest, dumbest person in the world. I was Razzy Gentry.

"Get off that tractor! Ain't you got a lick of sense?" said Papa. "Start picking up that tobacco before it goes to wilting."

Papa had been mad and embarrassed for having Razzy Gentry for a granddaughter.

I never learned how to back up a tractor. I was never allowed to get on one again.

* * *

"Come and eat you some lunch, Caroline," Granny yelled out the front door.

The kitchen smelled of fresh tomatoes and cucumbers. Suzanne hadn't returned yet, but Papa was already at the table. I washed up and sat down across from him.

"Did you water the dogs?" Papa asked.

"I will after I eat," I said. Papa just nodded. He always looked so angry, the left side of his face turned down in an eternal scowl because of the stroke. He finished his sandwich and rose with the help of his cane. He limped out of the kitchen, without a word, back to his recliner.

Ganny poured me some milk and sat down while I fixed my sandwich.

"Caroline, why don't you go check the peach trees today? I could make us a cobbler," she said with a sweet smile.

"Okay," I smiled back.

"But don't forget to water the dogs first," she half-whispered with a fake scowl. We both made a little giggle.

In The Pines

4

I grabbed a metal bucket from the shed and headed out to Nello Howard's old home place.

There wasn't a home there anymore, just a large stone foundation where the house used to be. I'd been going there as long as I could remember to pick peaches or apples from the old orchards. Papa told me the stone foundation was built by slaves. It was once the finest home place for miles around. I'd heard stories of its "once upon a time" magnificence all my life.

The aging house burned down before I was born. A vagrant's charred body was found in the ruins. Everyone figured he was trying to stay warm or cook. Maybe he fell asleep. Maybe he was drunk. Either way, he was dead, and so was the last genuine plantation between here and Wilmington.

There was evidence of the home's grand existence all around. Ancient oaks that once lined the home's drive still stood tall. Irises, buttercups, and tiger lilies bloomed here every spring, spotting the woods with bright colors. All the neighbors shared the peaches, apples, and pecans the plantation gave us.

I took a short cut across a sandy, barren field. The sun was so bright I could barely see.

I looked forward to the coolness of the forest. I entered the edge of the forest and could finally open my eyes. I heard a radio humming out some muffled music.

Tim Clayton's truck was backed into the woods. I would sneak past it so he wouldn't see me. I heard a girl laughing. Suzanne? I had to take a closer look.

Suzanne was sitting on the tailgate with a beer in her hand. Tim was kissing the back of her neck, making her giggle. Suzanne turned her head like she sensed I was there. She stared right into my eyes. I was turning to leave when Tim saw me.

"What the hell do you want?" Tim said. "You gettin' an eyeful?"

I just stood there like an idiot.

"I'm talking to you, you little freak," Tim said as he stepped toward me. I kept quiet.

He eyeballed me from head to toe and started laughing. He was laughing so hard he had to bend over and hold his knees.

"Suzy, are you sure you two are sisters? Or did the freak show come through town and leave her on your Ma's porch?" Suzanne started laughing. My eyes started burning.

"You go to hell, Tim Clayton," I heard myself say. Before I knew what I was doing, I swung my bucket hard and caught him across the jaw.

I watched as if in slow motion. Tim fell back, his hands reaching for his face. I dropped my bucket and ran like hell through the woods. Branches and briars stung my face, arms, and legs, but I kept running.

"I'll get you!" Tim yelled. "Everybody knows you're a weirdo. Everybody knows you ain't right in the head!"

I ran until Tim's ranting sounded like a faint echo. I reached the old plantation, sat on the rock foundation, and cried. The cuts and scratches burned, and my lungs felt hot.

I cried for a long time.

Maybe he was right. Maybe I wasn't right in the head. "You just think too much," Granny always told me.

I looked at my homemade shorts and shirt, made from bargain basement stripped cotton. My hair stayed kinky in the summer from the humidity. I'd pull it back in a pony tail, but before long a blonde halo of frizz formed around my head. Tim was right, I did look like a freak.

I forgot about the peaches. I wanted to walk. I wanted to get lost in the deepest, darkest part of the woods. I decided to go to Moccasin Branch.

In The Pines

5

Moccasin Branch was a part of the Cape Fear River that had decided to flow a few miles off on its own through the woods. It was a beautiful place. It had the look of a peaceful, inviting lagoon. If you sat quiet in the bushes, you could catch sight of a bobcat or deer playing in the water.

It was a dangerous place, too. It was home to the moccasin, a kind of poisonous snake. The snake had a head as big as a man's fist. Beyond the creek were dark and deadly swamps. Some people had seen alligators in there. Some say that at night you can hear the mournful wails of slaves who had died in the swamps. Lost souls.

I headed into the woods. I was mad, scared, and excited. I had never been to Moccasin without Papa.

The woods were thick. Everything was cold, wet, and green in this world of eternal shade. The old slave church loomed just ahead. It was weathered and gray, just a shell of a building. The floors inside had long ago fallen in and rotted away. Its rock foundation was exactly like the one at the Howard home. I stared at the building. The woods were so quiet—no bugs chirping, no birds singing—only the soft rustle of trees in the breeze.

I stood there for a few minutes, feeling at peace. I said "goodbye" out loud and continued my journey.

The woods were getting darker, the ground soft and squishy. I slowed down to watch for snakes. Several ducks took off flapping and squawking from the brush in front of me, making me jump in fright. I parted a thick bunch of cattails and could see the water. It was a deep dark blue, the color of the sky before a storm. It was as beautiful as I remembered.

I knelt down to watch as several cranes, taller than me, took stilted steps through the water. They were the color of pure snow. I stared off across the water into the blackness of the swamps. I don't know how long I sat there.

I strained my eyes to look as far into the darkness as I could.

Papa had been so excited the first time he had taken me here. It was as if he were giving me a gift. We had knelt in the brush with no words and took in the sights, sounds, and smells. I had watched Papa's face and could see something like delight in his eyes. We sat silent for a long time.

"Papa, what's on the other side?" I had asked.

"Another world, I think," was all he'd said.

"Sing 'In the Pines' for me Papa, please?" I'd asked.

"Why look at you! Your nose is red! Are you gettin' cold?" Papa had asked.

"I don't want to leave yet, Papa," I'd said.

"Come sit in my lap. I'll warm you up," he'd replied.

He had put me in his lap and wrapped his coat around me and sang softly in my ear. "In the pines, in the pines, where the sun never shines, and you shiver when the cold wind blows . . ."

The song came back to me now that I was out in Moccasin Branch again.

"In the pines, in the pines," I was singing to myself. The ancient moss, which hung thickly from the trees seemed to be gesturing to me, waving like limp hands. "Come in, come join us," the moss seemed to say. I had to look away.

I got up and ran until I made it back to the slave church. I was soaking wet with sweat. My cuts and scratches burned. I walked without stopping until I reached the clearing across from my house.

6

I walked to Papa's big barn without stopping. I found an old crate and stood on it and felt for the barn key above the door. Straining on my tiptoes, I ran my fingers across the rough board. The crate rocked slightly as my fingers ran through spider webs. Got it! I jumped off the crate before it fell.

I opened the double doors of the barn. Inside, there were two tractors, one big one and one small one. I found the key for the big tractor hanging on a nail. I hopped on the tractor. In just three licks and much smoke, it started. I revved the motor. It sounded good.

I hopped down and picked up the metal tongue of a long wooden trailer. I strained to roll it to the back of the tractor. I hooked it up to the tractor, no problem. My hair was drenched in sweat. I hopped back on the tractor and, after some work, put it into gear. I popped the clutch. With a jump like a bucking horse, the tractor took off.

I circled around the barn, knowing what I had to do. I would need to back the trailer into the spot where the tractor had been parked. Tight squeeze!

I pulled the tractor into position. I shifted in reverse. I was humming "In the Pines." I started backing up. The trailer started to swerve. "Just slow it down," I said to myself. "Easy does it."

I worked the steering wheel. Sweat dripped into my eyes. The trailer was cooperating. I kept going slowly until the trailer was backed perfectly into the vacant spot.

I stared for a moment at my accomplishment. I smiled.

"I knew I could do it!" I said out loud.

I pulled the trailer off the tractor, put everything back as I had found it, and headed home.

The late afternoon sun shone brightly, making our dingy white house shine like yellow gold.

The curtains were parted in the kitchen. I cupped my hands over my eyes. Papa was looking out. I stopped and stared back. He raised his hand in a slight wave. He smiled. I raised my hand back and smiled, too.

We stared at each other until the sun's glare took over and made my eyes water.

In The Pines

7

"My gracious! What happened to you?" Granny put her hands to her mouth when she saw me. My clothes were dirty and torn, my hair soaked from sweat. The blood from the scratches had dried, making them look a lot worse than they were.

"I've been worried sick! You've been gone all day," Granny said. "Look at you! What happened?"

I thought fast. "A wild dog chased me through the woods," I said. "I've been sitting in a deer stand all day, too scared to come down."

"You poor little thing," Granny said. "Come in the bathroom. Let me take a look at you. I'll run you a bath." Granny scurried to the bathroom, giving me several more "poor little things."

Papa was in his recliner, eyes closed. I stopped by his chair and looked down at him.

"I miss you, Papa" I whispered. He didn't move.

By nightfall, Suzanne still wasn't home. Granny, in her cotton nightgown, walked back and forth, staring at the door.

"Where is that girl?" she said to herself.

Granny was a beautiful woman. She had a soft presence that made you want to be near her. Growing up with her, I always knew that she would fight the devil himself to protect me. She had powder blue eyes and soft pink cheeks. Her hair was as white as the cranes at Moccasin Branch. She was sweet and strong and honest.

Granny had thought she'd go through life without a baby. She was almost forty before she conceived my mom. Granny was the happiest woman on earth. She and Papa hadn't had any idea how their world would be turned upside down.

Now, Papa sat in his recliner, going in and out of sleep. He was still dressed in his khaki work pants and shirt. His old green cap sat in anticipation on the end table beside him.

Granny, sweetly, oh so sweetly, coaxed him to go to bed as she did every night.

"Where's Iris at, by God? It's gettin' late," Papa said. (Iris was my mother's name).

"She'll be home soon . . . she is at a friend's house," Granny said softly. "Come on, daddy, let me help you to bed."

Papa, with the help of his cane and Granny, grabbed his cap and went to bed. Each night when he finally went to bed, Granny and I felt relief like letting out a huge breath of air. We felt free. We would pop popcorn and sit on the porch, sometimes shelling beans, sometimes just listening to the night. The evening air felt so cool and crisp. It made me smile.

"You know we won't keep Suzanne for much longer, don't you?" Granny said in a whisper.

"Yes, I know."

"She's just like her mother, just like her mother," said Granny.

We sat in silence. We heard the occasional thump of a frenzied moth hitting the porch screen. The bullfrogs and crickets seemed to compete, each growing louder and louder.

"Papa isn't himself now, you know. He can't help it. He's in pain." Granny rocked slowly as she spoke, the squeak of her chair like a soothing song. "Drinking is the only way he can deal with it. He feels useless," Granny whispered.

"Yes, ma'am, I know," I said.

I went to bed, and Granny looked in. We stared at each other, and she gave me a smile and turned away. Eventually, I heard Suzanne come creeping in the back door.

I closed my eyes and dreamed of the swamps. In my dream, I sailed silently over the black water, on the edge of darkness. I parted the thick moss like tattered curtains and stepped in.

The next morning, I'd rise before the sun. I always did. I'd feel at peace until the sky turned red as the hottest fire in hell and allowed the sun to burst through.

In The Pines

8

Papa died in his sleep on a cool October morning, just a few days before my fifteenth birthday. It was before sunrise, and Granny found me reading in my room. She came in and closed the door. I looked up and saw she was pale.

"What's wrong?" I asked.

"Papa's gone," she said.

She sat on my bed and stared into space. I took her hand and let her sit there in silence for several minutes. Her body slumped, and she sobbed.

"Oh, Harold," she said."Oh Harold, I'm so sorry." After a time, she sat her body straight and took several deep breaths. "I need to make some phone calls," she said. She gathered her strength and walked out the door.

My throat was tight, and my eyes burned. I was mostly crying for Granny. She was so sad. In a way, I was happy for Papa. His poor life had been so tortured the last few years. Now he was released.

The next few days were a whirlwind of food, prayers, and hugs, old ladies and bored men.

I found the number of the seafood restaurant where Suzanne was working at the beach, and I left her a message.

Suzanne showed up looking tan and beautiful. She had to be helped out of the church by several men because she was so distraught. I couldn't cry.

* * *

In the winter of my senior year, my Granny came to me and said, "I'm sick, Caroline."

She had pancreatic cancer. She grew thin and pale. I went to school and hoped health would take care of her until I got home.

"Oh, Caroline, go do your studies. I'm okay." She smiled. "I am going to be at your graduation. . . . You can count on that. I know you have always wanted to leave this farm. You need to have an education. I want you to have a good life."

"I will, Granny," I told her.

"Your Papa and I have money in savings at the bank. I have put it into an account for you. I want you to use it for college. I want you to sell the farm and split the money with Suzanne. Most important, Caroline, I want you to be happy." She smiled that sweet smile that was hers alone.

At graduation, Edna Thomas, the sweet, chubby, laughing home health nurse, wheeled my Granny to the front row of the auditorium.

"Excuse me, excuse me . . . VIP coming through!" shouted Edna, "Get outta my way people!"

Edna parked Granny front and center! Granny smiled and clapped softly when I received my high school diploma.

Mrs. Evangeline Louise Burns O'Dell, Granny, died four days later.

9

After Granny's funeral, Suzanne said, "We need to talk. What about this farm? What about my inheritance?"

"We will have to sell the place and split the money," I told her.

"How long will that take?" she asked.

"Who knows," I said.

"Well, I need the money, and you aren't getting it all," she said.

I turned and walked away.

I woke up the next morning and sat at the kitchen table.

I rifled through my acceptance letters from North Carolina State, Campbell College, and Western Carolina University. I opened the trash bin and dealt each letter into it. I took a shower and drove Papa's old truck into town.

When I returned, I heard Suzanne showering. I put on a pot of coffee and waited for her. She emerged wearing a robe and a towel on her head.

"Sit down," I said.

"I need to dry my hair."

"Not now," I said.

"What is wrong with you?" Suzanne sat down, rolling her eyes.

"I want to make a deal with you" I said.

"What are you talking about?" Suzanne said, acting agitated.

"Papa and Granny had a savings account. I withdrew it and had a cashier's check written for you. But, you have to promise that you will not try to get the farm, not the equipment, not the house."

Suzanne stared at me. "How much?" she asked.

I handed her the check. The check was the cumulative total of our grandparents' lives. The check was what was left of two beautiful, loving people. It was now in her hands.

"Thirty freaking thousand dollars?" she said. "Thirty freaking thousand dollars? Jesus Christ! Thirty freaking thousand dollars? Yes, yes, I'll take it!"

I thought her big brown eyes were going to pop right out of her head.

10

The summer after my graduation, I got a job at the county library. It was a good job. I enjoyed getting up and going there every day. I actually missed being there on my days off.

Being at the empty house was sometimes more than I could take. I would do my little bit of housekeeping, fix a small supper, and sit on the porch listening to the night. When it was hot, I'd take a shower, put on my nightgown, and sit on the porch with my hair still wet. This reminded me of my summer evenings with Rose.

It was quiet on the farm. I could hear the occasional car or truck go past. Their lights danced across the sandy fields.

Days turned to months, months to years. I worked every day. I came home from work every day. I had the occasional visit from Edna.

I had grown to love her dearly. She had taken such good care of Granny and brightened our dark days when she was so sick.

"Girl, what are you doing?" she'd say. "You need to get out and socialize. You are young and pretty and smart. You gonna waste away up here on this old farm. Come out with me and my girls. Come on!"

I'd laugh and say no thanks. She could make me laugh so hard.

"They's some fine looking men at the club. . . . You need to go with us!"

"Edna, you're so crazy," I'd reply.

One Friday in the month of October, I came home from work and immediately noticed an old, beat up car parked at my house.

"What the hell?" I said to myself. Suzanne came out on the porch smiling at me.

"Caroline!" she shouted. She ran and hugged me. She was wearing tight-fitting jeans and a crisp white blouse. She smelled of perfume, and her dark hair was cut in a slanted bob.

"Suzanne?" I said. "I almost thought you were dead."

"Don't be silly," she said. "Why look at you, Caroline! You are so pretty!"

I wanted to take this as a compliment. I had learned to tame my curly hair. I had my Granny's petite figure, and I now wore a little mascara on my blonde eyelashes.

"Thank you, Suzanne. You look pretty as always."

"Oh hush your mouth," she said and gave a silly gush.

"So, what brings you here?" I asked.

"Well," she said, "I want you to meet your niece."

"My niece?"

Suzanne went into the house. I followed. There on my couch was a tiny little being. She had curly, dark auburn hair. Her face was soft and round. She was balled up like a kitten. She had Granny's old bed quilt wrapped around her.

"My niece? You mean . . . your daughter?" I whispered.

"Yes, my daughter. This is Rachel."

"What? When? Are you serious, Suzanne?" I asked.

"Well, she's twenty-three months now," said Suzanne. "It's not been easy, you know, trying to work and take care of a baby. Oh my God! I thought I would die!"

With a look of disbelief, I just stared from Suzanne to the little being. What could I say?

"Oh, don't you judge me, Caroline," said Suzanne. "You have it made, sitting up here free and clear on this farm. I can't believe how you swindled me in my time of grief. You think you are so smart."

"I didn't swindle you, Suzanne, and you know it. Why are you here? What do you want?"

"Okay, okay," she said. "I get so emotional when I'm here. I'm sorry, okay? I just miss them so much." She started to cry.

"What do you want, Suzanne?" I asked.

"Well, you are just cold hearted," she said.

"No, I'm not," I said. "I just know you."

She dried her eyes and stared at me.

"Alright," she took a deep breath. "I need you to keep Rachel a couple of weeks. I met this man. . . . He's wonderful. He's a businessman. He has money. He wants to take me on a cruise!"

"I work, Suzanne, every day. What would I do with her?" I asked.

"Oh, I'm sure one of those fat, bored moms around here would just love to keep her!" said Suzanne.

I sat and thought a few minutes.

"What would you do with her if I said no?" I asked.

She looked to the floor and back to me."I truly don't know," she said.

In a few minutes, Rachel and I were on the porch, waving goodbye.

"Rachel, mama loves you!" Suzanne shouted from the car window before she drove off.

When all was quiet, Rachel said, "I poo poo." She pointed to her rear.

"Oh my God," I said.

* * *

About a month later, I heard from Suzanne, on a small postcard in the mail.

Hi all! I'm in Greece. It's beautiful here. Sorry to be gone so long. Give Rachel hugs and kisses! Will be home soon. Love, Suzanne

In the back of my mind, I had known this would happen. I had known it as soon as I saw her car leave my drive.

I was quite amazed at how seldom Rachel ever mentioned her mother. In fact, not one tear had been shed for her. Her transition to life with me on the farm and her new daycare had gone very smoothly. It seemed as if she were meant to be here with me.

We painted her room (Suzanne's old room) a pretty powder blue. She picked the color out herself. I got her a bedspread, pillow shams, and curtains to match. They were white with beautiful blue irises on them. She loved her room.

In the suitcase that came with her there were a few crumpled up dresses, t-shirts, and pants that were too small. I have to admit that I enjoyed shopping for her new clothes. She loved dresses and tights the most. She loved lacy nightgowns and shiny shoes. She loved stuffed animals and baby dolls.

She was growing more beautiful every day.

In The Pines

11

It was near the end of April. I sat little Rachel down at the kitchen table.

"We have to have an important talk," I told her.

"Okay," she said, looking quite curious.

"It is time we decide what we are going to plant in our garden this spring. I need you to tell me what you want to grow."

"Can we grow flowers, Caroline?"

"Yes, we can grow flowers . . . but what about vegetables?"

"Veg-ables!" she clapped.

"You like corn," I said. "You like green beans and cucumbers.

"Yes!" she yelled.

"What else do you want?"

"Apples, please!" That made me laugh.

After breakfast, we went to the feed and seed to shop. We both loved going there. Two big, fat cats lounged lazily around the store. A short and stubby corgi dog begged for petting. They were pleasant fixtures at the store. Rachel went straight to the big, colorful display of flower seeds.

"Pretty," she said.

"Pick out a few," I told her. I felt a tap on my shoulder and turned around.

There stood a tall, blonde, handsome man.

"Excuse me ma'am, are you Caroline O'Dell?"

"Yes," I said.

"Do you remember me?" he asked.

I looked him up and down. "I do . . . I think," I said.

"Oh? Well I think of you every day, Miss Caroline." With that he lifted his chin and showed me a good two-inch scar.

My eyes grew big.

"It is Miss, isn't it?" he asked.

"Ah, yes," I said.

"Don't worry," he said. "I deserved it." He gave a sweet, genuine grin.

"Tim Clayton," I said. "Wow. I mean, ah, I don't know what I mean." I half giggled like a silly schoolgirl. "I'm sorry," I said.

He laughed, "Sorry to bother you."

"Oh no, it's okay."

"Caroline, I want these!" Rachel handed me several seed packs. I looked over at the display, and it was destroyed.

"And who is this pretty little thing?" Tim Clayton asked.

"My niece," I said. "This is Rachel."

He looked at her and back at me.

"Yes," I said. "Suzanne's little girl. She's beautiful like her mama."

"I don't know," Tim said. "She's got her aunt's beautiful curls."

My hand went straight to my hair. "Well, thank you." I smiled.

"Are you still living at the farm?" he asked.

"Of course I am," I said.

"Caroline, Caroline, come see!" Rachel yelled.

"Gotta go," I said. "The queen beckons."

"Good to see you, Caroline."

"Good to see you, too, Tim."

Later that week I was working at the library, restocking shelves with returned books. I was trying to get out as soon as possible so I could pick up Rachel.

"Ma'am, I'm looking for a book," someone said.

"Just what kind of book are you looking for?" I asked.

"Well," he grinned. "A book about how to ask out a beautiful woman that I once treated so badly."

"Hmm, I suppose you would have to ask this person and her niece out," I said.

"Oh?" said Tim. "Where would this person and her niece like to go?"

"We like burgers and ice cream."

"Is there a special a place that you like to eat said burgers and ice cream?" he asked.

"Nope, we're not picky."

"I will pick you ladies up at seven on Saturday night," Tim said.

"You better make it six. Rachel's bedtime is eight," I said.

"Six it is, Caroline."

12

"Girl, you got a date!" Edna screamed, bouncing Rachel in her lap. "You know I would keep this baby for you."

"I know," I said, "but I want her to go, too."

"You just don't want to be alone with such a fine looking man, and lord knows, I don't know why," said Edna.

"Caroline, I want to stay with Ed-ma," Rachel said.

"Not tonight, baby girl," I said. I gave Edna a sideways look.

"So, what you gonna wear, Caroline?"

"I guess just jeans and a t-shirt."

"A V-neck, a low-cut? she asked.

"Stop!" I laughed.

"You gotta give up a little skin, girl! What are you, a nun?"

"What's a nun, Ed-ma?" Rachel asked.

Tim's big truck came slowly up the drive, ten minutes early. I liked that. He got out of the car, and Rachel ran out. I stayed back, waiting for him to come to the door.

"Caroline, Caroline, he's here!" she shouted.

"I know, I know," I said. Tim came in with Rachel holding his hand.

"I can honestly say that I have never been welcomed so warmly into someone's home," Tim said with a big smile. I smiled, too.

That evening, we went to a local burger place with a playground for children. Rachel loved it! She played and laughed and made many new friends.

Tim brought us home and carried a sleeping Rachel to bed. We sat on the top step of the porch and listened to the night.

He put his arm around me and asked, "What are you going to do with this farm?"

"I haven't really thought about it," I said. We sat in silence a little longer.

"You know," he said, "there's a big strawberry farm over in Harnett County . . . they do good. People come from all over to get strawberries there. You could do that."

"Strawberries," I said. "Rachel loves strawberries." Tim grinned and got up and walked around the front yard. He pointed to the big barn across the field.

"You could make that barn a greenhouse for your plants. The big field over there could be your initial field. It would work!"

"You think?" I said.

"Okay," he said. "I've got a degree from North Carolina State in agriculture. I did learn more than how to make a beer can pyramid while I was there." He grinned.

That summer, Rachel, Tim, and I had the most beautiful vegetable and flower garden in the county. Tim plowed one whole side just for Rachel's flowers. He helped her plant every seed. She loved watching her flowers grow, and Tim and I loved watching her grow.

We three spent every minute we could together. He was busy on his farm, and I at the library, but when we were free, we would swim in the creek and lie in the sun. We grilled out and played tag.

We would laugh and run and scream. Some nights he would pitch a tent in the yard and build a fire. We'd stay out and tell stories and roast marshmallows.

The summer was turning to fall and Tim asked me to marry him.

"Yes!" I said.

I was keeping my promise to Granny. I was happy.

13

It is amazing how time ticks by on this sandy land. The day after Tim proposed, Rachel was going to kindergarten. She looked way too tiny to be going to school. She was so excited.

"I'll take you on your first day. I don't mind," I said.

"Nope, I want to ride the bus!" she said, jumping up and down. She had watched the big, yellow bus drive by our house ever since she could remember. She couldn't wait to get on it.

"Okay, okay, do you remember where to go?"

Rachel bobbed her head up and down at least ten times. "Yes, yes, yes!" Rachel skipped the whole way down our long, sandy drive, singing, "I'm going to school! I'm going to school!" She had to use her hands to help boost herself up the giant steps of the bus. She got to the top and stood and stared at Miss Judy, the bus driver.

"Go find you a place to sit," Miss Judy said. Rachel glanced back at me, suddenly looking nervous. I smiled and waved. Rachel waved back and took a seat behind Miss Judy.

Whoosh! The big doors shut, and off they went. I cried the whole way back to the house.

Time passes much too quickly when you are happy.

14

"Caroline? Is this you?" A voice said through the telephone.

"Yes, who is this?" I asked.

"It's your sister, silly. It's Suzanne!" I was silent. "How is Rachel?" she asked.

"She started kindergarten yesterday," I said.

"Caroline, I knew she would be good with you," said Suzanne. "I knew you would do her right. You know?" Her voice cracked.

"I love her, Suzanne," I said. A few seconds passed.

"Caroline, I'm sorry." Suzanne sounded sincere. "I'm living in Rhode Island now. I have a son. My husband is so good to us, Caroline. He's a good provider. He doesn't know about Rachel."

"Thank you for bringing her to me, Suzanne," I said. "I mean that from the bottom of my heart."

"Thank you, Caroline." The connection went dead.

It was a Sunday after church time. I drove over to where Edna lived. Her street had several little lanes of small wood frame houses with neat lawns.

I saw Edna sitting on her Mama's porch. She lived next door in her Grandma's old house. She and her mama were dressed in their Sunday best, each sitting in a rocking chair. I pulled in the drive.

"Well, look what the cat's drug up! Caroline O'Dell! How're you, girl?" Edna was dressed in a bright yellow dress that buttoned down the front. Those buttons looked stressed, like they were going to pop off. Her Mama was in a soft lavender suit with a cream colored blouse.

"Where's that baby girl?" Edna asked.

"She's with Tim," I said. "She's been asking for a sand box, and he reminded her that she had the world's biggest sand box right by her yard. So, when I left they were building a dirt castle."

"Oh, my goodness! What a sweet child, and what a sweet man!" Edna said. "Get up here and have a seat."

"It sure is good to see you, Caroline," Mrs. Thomas said. "You should bring that baby to church with us."

"I know. I should," I said. I just didn't hold much to church. The yelling preacher had scared me to death as a child. My Papa would say, "There's more sinners in a church than on the street."

The phone rang in the house, and Mrs. Thomas went to answer.

"Edna, I have something to ask of you," I said.

"You look so serious. What you need, little girl?"

"I want you to be my maid of honor. Tim asked me to marry him."

"What? Lord have mercy! You gettin' married! Woohoo!" she yelled and clapped her hands and stomped her feet.

Mrs. Thomas came out on the porch. "Edna, quit being so damn loud on my porch. It's Sunday," she said.

"She's getting married, Mama!" shouted Edna.

"Well, bless your heart," Mrs. Thomas said. "Now, hush up out here, Edna." Edna and I laughed until we cried.

"I would love to be your maid of honor, Caroline. How many bridesmaids you having?"

"Just you, Edna," I said.

"Just me?" she said. "I get to pick out my own dress, right? When you have this—she pointed down to her body—you've got to flaunt it. You would have me dressed like a pilgrim. I know you would."

"Okay, you pick out your dress," I said, "but steer clear of hot pink or bright red."

"You are no fun, Caroline. You know, you are the only woman I ever knew who could honestly wear a white dress at her wedding."

I got up to leave and walked to my car.

"By the way," I said with a big smile, "I will be wearing an off-white dress."

"What?" Edna yelled. "You are honestly leaving me with that? Get back up here!"

I waved bye and got in my car. Edna was laughing and yelling. Mrs. Thomas came back out on the porch. I saw her wagging her finger at Edna. Edna just laughed.

The next morning, I woke up before the sun came up. I took my coffee to the back step and sat and watched the red sky.

I could see Tim's truck at the barn. I could hear beating and banging. My greenhouse was being built.

I didn't hate the sunrise any longer. I knew it would be the time that Rachel, with her crazy hair and sleepy eyes, would climb onto my lap. It would be the time that Tim would get up and kiss both our brows and get ready to work.

I stared out across the fields and knew I would never leave this place. That knowledge felt so good and right and warm. I smiled.

About The Author

Jennie Ford is a mother, writer, potter, and artist. Jennie was raised in Eastern North Carolina, where the rich farming landscapes provide the backdrop to many of her stories.

As a contributor to Storyshares for many years, she will continue to compose short stories for their expanding library. Now residing in Western North Carolina, Jennie is currently writing a novel for young adult readers, which she hopes to publish in the future.

About The Publisher

Story Shares is a nonprofit focused on supporting the millions of teens and adults who struggle with reading by creating a new shelf in the library specifically for them. The ever-growing collection features content that is compelling and culturally relevant for teens and adults, yet still readable at a range of lower reading levels.

Story Shares generates content by engaging deeply with writers, bringing together a community to create this new kind of book. With more intriguing and approachable stories to choose from, the teens and adults who have fallen behind are improving their skills and beginning to discover the joy of reading. For more information, visit storyshares.org.

Easy to Read. Hard to Put Down.

In The Pines

www.ingramcontent.com/pod-product-compliance
Lightning Source LLC
Chambersburg PA
CBHW072232190626
46809CB00017B/1891